# GOLDIE THE UNICORN

## Mary K. Smith

ISBN-13: 978-1535274265
ISBN-10: 1535274263

# DEDICATION

This book is dedicated to my children. It is my deepest wish that these stories bring back special memories from childhood.

*"I love you to the moon and back."*
-Mom

# CONTENTS

# ACKNOWLEDGMENTS

Believe in yourself. Don't let others tell you what you
are capable of. Think big and follow your dreams.
The dreamers of the world make big things happen.

# Goldie the Unicorn

Let me tell you a story about a small fairy named Angie and her best friend, Goldie the unicorn. When the other fairies would fly away to their work, Angie would stay back and look after the beautiful pink castle they lived in. The castle had pink heart shaped windows and pink colored flags with pink hearts on it.

Angie would get up every morning and look out of her window and see the blue birds flying past her window. The bees would be buzzing on the yellow flowers. Angie used to fly out of her window and join the birds and sing along with them.

She would sit with the bees on flowers and smell them. Ah such a lovely smell! One day Angie was busy decorating flowers in her room when she heard a noise outside her window. She saw a small unicorn lost and crying. Angie was very worried and flew down to the unicorn.

"What is the matter little unicorn?" asked Angie. "Why are you crying? Are you lost?"

The small unicorn looked up at the fairy, stopped crying and stared in surprise. "You can fly? Wow! How I wish I had wings? You have such a nice pair of wings!"

Angie laughed and said, "Oh my dear unicorn, do you know it is so much hard work to keep the wings clean and protect them from harm? But tell me your name and why were you crying."

The small unicorn said, "My name is Goldie because I am golden in color and my parents love me a lot. They have gone on a holiday and left me behind with my brothers and sisters at my aunt's house. All of us have been playing in the morning and while playing I discovered a small pink flower. I went in search of more pink flowers but then I realized I was far away from my brothers and my sisters. I started searching for them but couldn't find them. I was lost! Then I saw your pink castle and was waiting for them but no one has come in search of me."

Goldie was sad again but Angie said, "Oh don't worry. Once the big fairies are back from work we will find your family for you! I promise!"

Goldie was happy to hear that and smiled the loveliest smile.

Angie said, "I am feeling hungry. Let's have breakfast and then wait for the fairies to come back."

So both of them went inside the pink castle and Angie showed Goldie her small room. Goldie was in love with the room! The room had pink curtains that blew in the wind, a small heart shaped window where you could see the whole countryside, the bed had soft cushions and Angie and Goldie jumped on the bed for a long, long time and completely forgot to have their breakfast! They rushed down to have breakfast and Angie made yummy sandwiches of cheese, chocolate milkshakes and a nice big serving of strawberry ice cream!

They enjoyed their breakfast and after that Angie took Goldie out to play. They ran though rows of flowers and were careful not to hurt them. They jumped over puddles of water and splashed water on each other.

Goldie was careful not to splash water on Angie's wings.

Angie then took Goldie to such a wonderful place. A beautiful seven colored rainbow! Angie flew on top of the rainbow and sat on it and called out to Goldie, "Goldie come and join me!"

Now how could Goldie join Angie? Goldie tried to climb the rainbow but couldn't. The rainbow was slippery and every time Goldie would try to climb up, she would slip down. Angie caught hold of Goldie and flew her to the top of the rainbow.

Such a beautiful sight! "I can see everyone and everything!" shouted Goldie. "But I cannot see my family. Oh how I wish they were here." And Goldie was sad again. But Angie told Goldie not to be sad and reminded her that the fairies will help Goldie get back to her family.

After they had fun sitting on the rainbow, Angie asked the rainbow if it could please take Goldie and her back to the castle as they were very tired. The rainbow smiled and took the two of them back to the pink castle. Both of them fell asleep and slept until evening. It was time for the fairies to return home and Angie was eagerly waiting for the fairies to come back and tell them the whole story. The fairies came back from work and were surprised to see a golden unicorn in their castle.

"Who are you? What is your name, dear unicorn?" asked the fairies. Angie told them the whole story and then asked if the fairies could help. The fairies said yes they would and Angie and Goldie were so happy to hear that. The fairies searched far and near around the place till they found other unicorns and asked if they were missing a small unicorn. Goldie was taken back to her family and how happy she was!

Angie was very happy for Goldie and made Goldie promise her that she would come with her brothers and sisters and play with Angie. Goldie promised that she would and was sad to see Angie leave. Before Angie left she gave Goldie a gift. She made a small heart shaped crystal for Goldie and told her to always carry the crystal with her.

If ever she got lost, she only had to ask the heart crystal and it would take her home. Goldie was happy to have such a nice gift and thanked Angie. They said goodbye and Goldie always remembered the kind fairy that had helped her that day and promised to see her soon, very soon!

# Maze #1

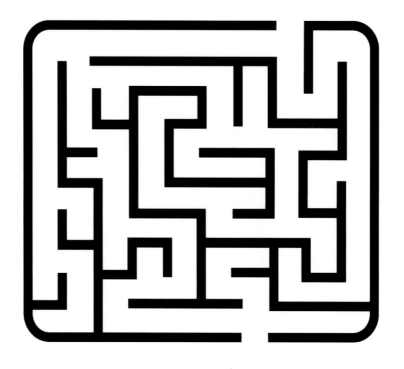

# Maze #2

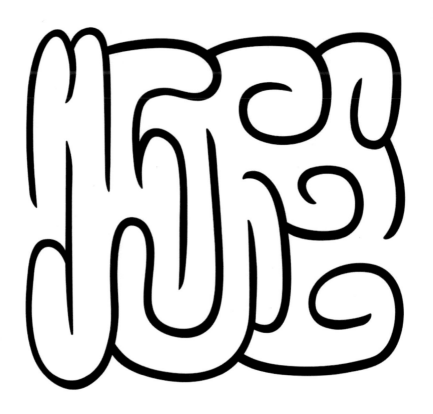

# Maze #3

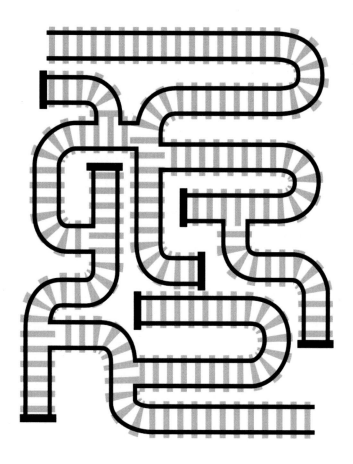

# Maze #4

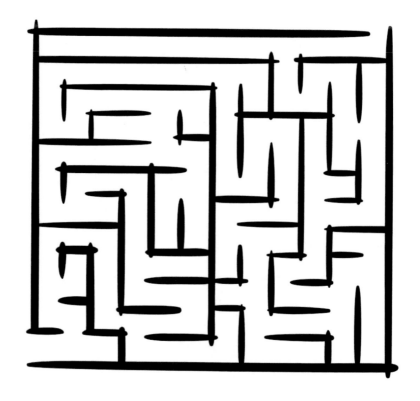

# Maze #5

# Maze #6

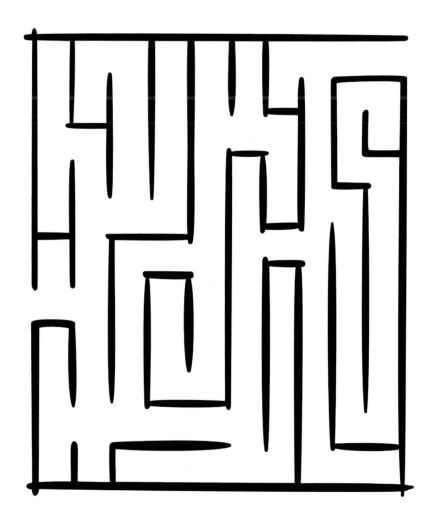

# Maze #7

# Maze #8

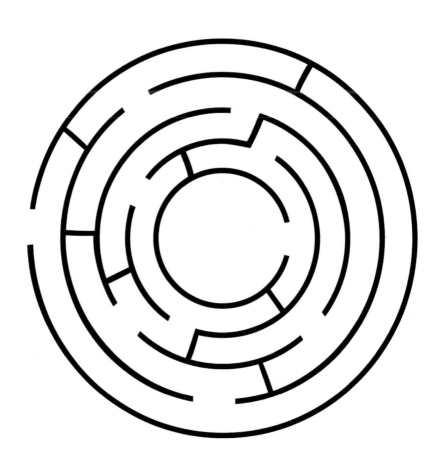

# Maze Solutions 1-4

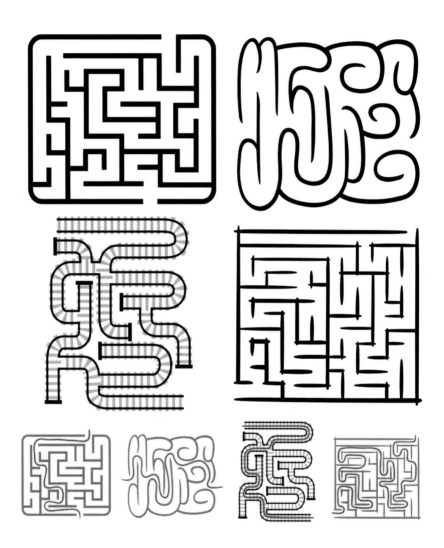

# Maze Solutions 5-8

# ABOUT THE AUTHOR

Mary K. Smith is a mother, a storyteller, and a kid at heart. During her childhood, her grandmother filled her imagination about stories of unicorns, fairies, and princesses. Those stories found a special place in her heart as she told those same stories to her children. As her children grew up and had their own children, they shared those stories with their children, and now Mary shares those same stories with the world.

*"Think big. Live your dreams!"*
Mary K. Smith